For everyone who knows one,
or who is a bit of a Harriet.
P.K.

First published 2019 by Two Hoots
an imprint of Pan Macmillan
20 New Wharf Road, London N1 9RR
Associated companies throughout the world
www.panmacmillan.com
ISBN 978-1-5098-6722-6
Text and illustrations copyright © Puck Koper 2019
Moral rights asserted.

1 3 5 7 9 8 6 4 2
A CIP catalogue record for this book is available from the British Library.
Printed in China

www.twohootsbooks.com

WHERE IS YOUR SISTER?

PUCK KOPER

TWO HOOTS

It's Saturday and Mum, Harriet and I are going shopping.
I don't like shopping. Department stores are okay,
but only because they have cafés with cake.

First you have to survive the ground floor. It's full of fancy
ladies with smelly perfumes. Holding your breath is the only way!

"We need to get a new saucepan," says Mum.
"And cake!" I say.
"No, honey, we don't have time for cake today,
maybe next time."

"What if we hurry and get the saucepan really quickly?

Then we'd have time for some scones in the café, or carrot cake . . .

Hmmmm, maybe a Chelsea bun would be nice. Oh wait, no, some chocolate cake! Yes, chocolate cake! Or maybe some . . ."

"WHERE IS YOUR SISTER?"

"She's over there, Mum!" I say.

Silly Harriet, this way we won't have time for cake at all!

FITTING ROOMS →

Mum runs after her. I try to keep up but she is quite fast.

"Excuse me!"

"I'm terribly sorry!"

"Pardon me!"

I'm not sure why Mum is so upset.

"She's just over there," I tell her.

But it doesn't seem to help.

We go to every floor, chasing after Harriet.
Everyone joins in. I think it's all quite exciting!
But Mum doesn't look excited at all.

"Ladies and gentlemen, today
we have a special offer on cakes in our café.
All the cakes are ha—"

"HAR

Now everyone is looking at us.
How embarrassing!

This way we'll never get any cake!

Suddenly Mum flies forward . . .

. . . and stops.

Harriet, at last!

At first there is some yelling . . .

. . . but soon it's all good.

So good that Mum takes us for cake to celebrate.

Harriet goes for the apple pie, I pick the chocolate cake.

It is even better than I remembered.

"We'll have to come back for that saucepan on Monday," says Mum, "And I saw a dress I'd like to try on, too."